Shen Roddie was born in Singapore. She graduated with a degree
in history and began her career as a journalist, interviewing the first
men to land on the moon. She lived in Buenos Aires, Argentina and Holland
before settling back in Oxford. Shen's previous books include *Shipwreck!* and
Fancy That (Victoria House), *Henry's Box* (Ladybird) and,
for Frances Lincoln, *Toes are to Tickle*.

Sally Anne Lambert grew up in Crosby, Liverpool. Her first book, *The Ginger
Bread Man* (Pavilion), was commissioned while she was still a student at
Lanchester University, Coventry, where she graduated with a BA Hons in
graphic design. Her most recent title for Frances Lincoln is
Hippety-hop, Hippety-hay, written by Opal Dunn.

For Aimee, Aileen and Dawn · S.R.
For Katie, Jonny, Sophie and Amy · S.A.L.

First published in Great Britain in 1997 by
Frances Lincoln Limited, 4 Torriano Mews
Torriano Avenue, London NW5 2RZ

First paperback edition 1998

British Library Cataloguing in Publication Data
available on request

ISBN 0-7112-1162-0 hb
ISBN 0-7112-1226-0 pb

Set in Berkeley

Printed in Hong Kong

3 5 7 9 8 6 4

Best of Friends!

Shen Roddie

Illustrated by Sally Anne Lambert

FRANCES LINCOLN

Hippo and Pig were neighbours. They lived
in a winding lane with a tall green hedge
between their houses.

On Mondays, Wednesdays and Fridays,
Hippo waddled over to Pig's house for
peppermint tea and chocolate doughnuts.

On Tuesdays, Thursdays and Saturdays,
Pig trotted over to Hippo's for a cool mud-bath.

One Sunday, the day when they stayed at home,
Pig decided to knit Hippo a scarf.

"It'll be finished just in time for his birthday,"
said Pig, and started to knit.

That same Sunday, Hippo decided to do something nice and neighbourly for Pig.

"I'll cut down the hedge between us," he thought. "Then we can see into each other's houses and really be friends." He got out his shears, climbed up a ladder and began to clip the hedge.

"SNIP, SNIP, SNIP!" went the shears.

"WOBBLE, WOBBLE, WOBBLE!" went the ladder.

The tall green hedge got shorter and shorter.

"Wallowing walruses!" exclaimed Hippo, peering over the hedge. "I can see Pig in her house. She's knitting a scarf. I bet it's a present for my birthday!"

Hippo hurried into his house.
  "I'd better make a present for Pig," he said,
and he got out his modelling clay.

Just then, Pig looked up from her knitting.

"Fluttering flamingos!" exclaimed Pig.
"The hedge has shrunk!"
Pig stared right into Hippo's house.
"He's making a mug with a pig on it.
I'm sure it's a present for my birthday!"

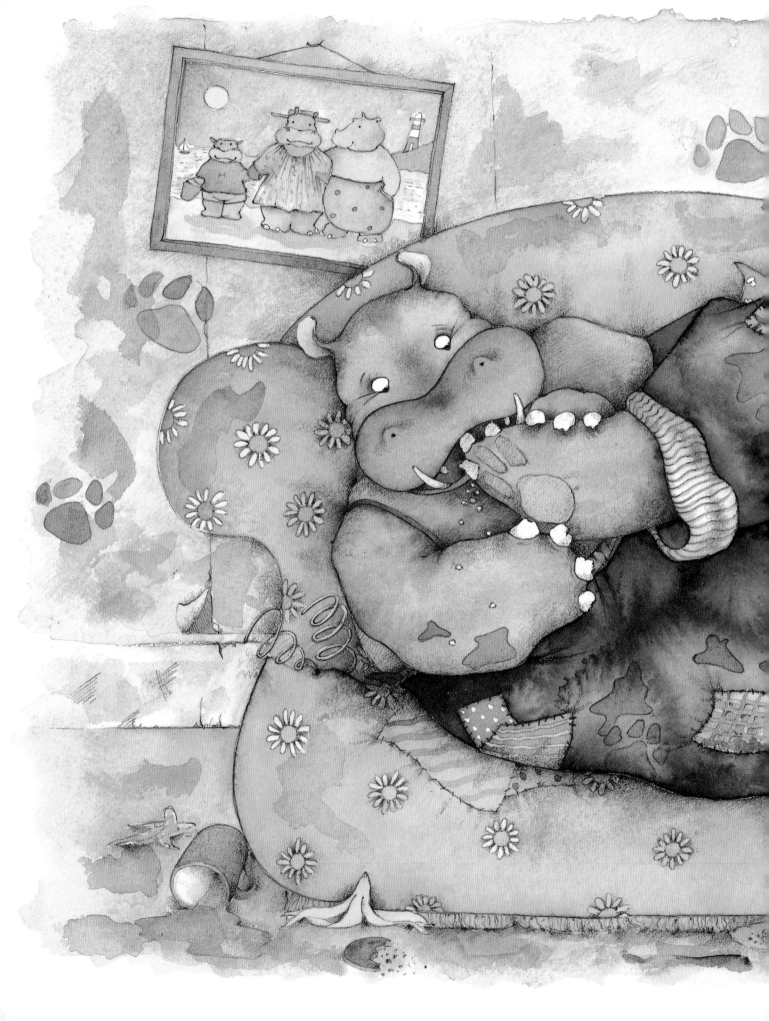

As Pig watched, Hippo waddled into another room and flopped on to a settee. He started chewing his toe-nails - all sixteen of them.
"Revolting!" thought Pig.

Then Hippo went off to cook lunch.
As he cooked, he kept licking the ladle
and putting it back in the pot.

"UGH!" shrieked Pig in horror,
as she thought of all the bowls of soup
she had drunk at Hippo's house.

Pig had seen quite enough. She needed a snack.
Hippo looked up and saw Pig through the window.
As he watched, Pig pounced on a pile of cream buns . . .

. . . and stuffed them all down in one go!
It made Hippo feel sick.

"Time for some exercise," said Pig,
belching loudly.

"Dancing is *very* good exercise,"
said Pig, as she sucked in her breath
to button her tutu.

She whirled, and she twirled,
then . . .

SNAP! The tutu burst and Pig
fell flat on her face.

Hippo roared with laughter. He had
never seen Pig look so funny.

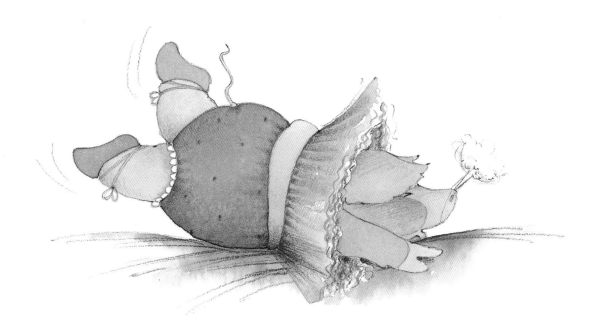

Pig heard Hippo chuckling and looked out of her window.

"Hippo!" shouted Pig. "Are you watching me?"

"Yes, Pig!" answered Hippo. "You were gorging cream buns and falling flat on your face."

Pig blushed.

"Well," she said, "you were chewing your toe-nails and licking your soup ladle."

"**YOU WERE WATCHING ME!**" they cried.
"**NO I WASN'T!**" they shouted.
"**YES YOU WERE!**" they yelled.

Pig drew her pink curtains.
Hippo pulled down his green blinds.

After that, Pig and Hippo stopped seeing
each other.

    Every day, Pig drank peppermint tea
alone in her garden . . .

Every day, Hippo took
a mud-bath all by himself.
Meanwhile, the hedge
grew back tall and green.

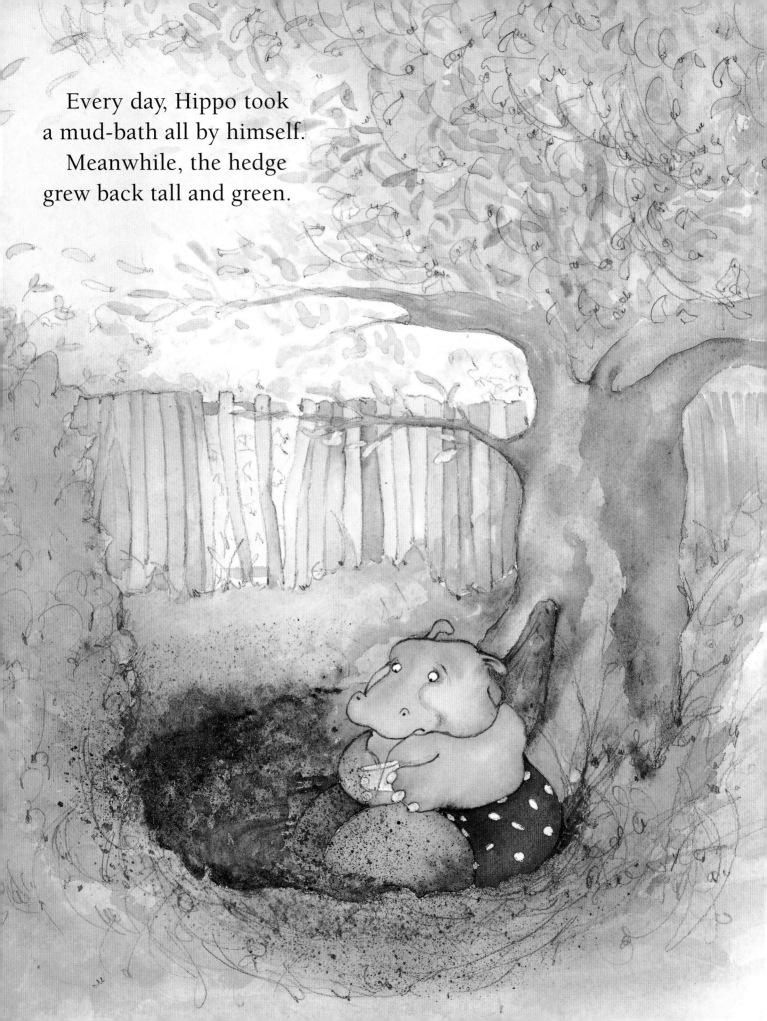

At last, it was Hippo's birthday.

    Pig picked up the scarf she had knitted
and crept over to Hippo's house.

    "Happy birthday, Hippo!" she said shyly.

    "Oh Pig, what a *lovely* surprise. Thank you,"
Hippo said, as he unwrapped the scarf. "I have
a present for you, too, but you'll have to wait
until *your* birthday. You'll never guess what it is!"

    They both laughed . . .

And as it was a Monday, Hippo went back
to Pig's house for peppermint tea, chocolate
doughnuts and a special iced cake.

Pig and Hippo were the best of friends again.
But ever after, back in their own homes . . .

. . . they did . . .

exactly as they pleased!

MORE PICTURE BOOKS IN PAPERBACK
FROM FRANCES LINCOLN

TOES ARE TO TICKLE
Shen Roddie
Illustrated by Kady MacDonald Denton

'A puddle is to jump in. A handbag is to empty.' Children's first discoveries
about the world around them are expressed with humour and sensitivity
in this delightful book.

Suitable for Nursery Level; and for National Curriculum English – Reading, Key Stage 1
ISBN 0-7112-1112-4

ELEPHANTS DON'T DO BALLET
Penny McKinlay
Illustrated by Graham Percy

When Esmeralda the elephant wants to be a ballerina, Mummy's not so sure –
after all, elephants don't do ballet. But Esmeralda *always* gets what she wants,
so she joins a ballet class...

Suitable for National Curriculum English – Reading, Key Stage 1
Scottish Guidelines English Language – Reading, Level A
ISBN 0-7112-1130-2

THE SNOWCHILD
Debi Gliori

Poor left-out Katie doesn't know how to play. She has lots of good ideas –
but she's always out of step with the other children's games. Then, one winter's
morning, Katie wakes up and decides to build a snowman...

Suitable for National Curriculum English - Reading, Key Stages 1 and 2
Scottish Guidelines English Language - Reading, Levels A and B
ISBN 0-7112-0894-8

Frances Lincoln titles are available from all good bookshops